CHARLIE & MOUSE
ARE MAGIC

By **LAUREL SNYDER**   Illustrated by **EMILY HUGHES**

chronicle books · san francisco

For Mose and Lewis, who have always been magic to me —L. S.

Library of Congress Cataloging-in-Publication Data available.

ISBN 978-1-4521-8341-1

Manufactured in China.

MIX
Paper from
responsible sources
FSC™ C104723
FSC
www.fsc.org

Design by Mariam Quraishi.
Typeset in Baskerville.
The illustrations in this book were rendered
by hand in graphite and with Photoshop.

10 9 8 7 6 5 4 3 2 1

Chronicle Books LLC
680 Second Street
San Francisco, California 94107

Chronicle Books—we see things differently. Become part of our community at www.chroniclekids.com.

Contents

MAGIC

Mom was in the kitchen.

Mouse was in the kitchen, too.

"Mouse!" said Mom. "You are making a mess."

"Mom!" said Mouse. "*You* are making a mess."

"I am not just making a mess," said Mom. "I am making dinner."

"Well," said Mouse, "I am not just making a mess either. I am making a potion. It is a magic potion."

"Oh," said Mom. "I did not see that you were

making a magic potion."

"I know," said Mouse.

"When will you be done?" asked Mom.

"I need to finish dinner."

"Soon," said Mouse.

Mouse added a pinch of salt.

Mom waited.

Mouse added two squirts of dish soap.

Mom waited.

Mouse stirred the magic potion.

Mom waited.

He stirred it SLOWLY.

Mom waited.

"Now," said Mouse, "I will put a drop of

potion on my nose and make a wish."

Mouse put a drop of potion on his nose.

Mouse waited. Mom waited.

Mouse waited some more.

"Mouse," said Mom.

"I would really like to

finish dinner. Do you think

if I gave you a cookie, you could

wait in the other room?"

"Mom!" shouted Mouse. "Wow! I CAN'T

BELIEVE IT!"

"What?" said Mom. "What can't you believe?"

"A cookie is EXACTLY what I was wishing for.

Isn't that amazing? My potion works!"

"Amazing!" said Mom. "Now scram."

"Hey," said Charlie.

"How did you get a cookie?"

"*Magic*!" said Mouse.

"Magic?"

asked Charlie.

"*Scram*!" said Mom.

Charlie and Mouse

scrammed.

INVISIBLE

"Mom is in a *mood*," said Mouse. "I wonder why."

"I am in a *mood*, too," said Charlie. "Because I

am covered in glop."

"That is not glop," said Mouse. "That is my potion."

"What will your potion do to me?" asked Charlie.

"That remains to be seen," said Mouse.

"Also, it is no fair that you got a cookie,"

said Charlie.

"You can have half of my cookie," said Mouse.

"It is not a very big half," said Charlie.

"But thank you."

Charlie and Mouse munched their cookies.

After a while, Tess and Lottie walked past.

Charlie and Mouse waved.

Tess and Lottie did not wave back.

Mr. Eric and Mr. Michael jogged past.

Charlie and Mouse waved.

Mr. Eric and Mr. Michael did not look.

"Mouse," said Charlie. "I think maybe we are invisible."

"Yes," said Mouse, nodding. "We are probably invisible."

"Interesting," said Charlie.

"You know," said Mouse, "when you are invisible you can make silly faces at people, and they will not even notice."

"Let's try it!" said Charlie.

A car drove past the house.

Charlie and Mouse made silly faces.

The car did not stop.

"When you are invisible," said Charlie, "you can shout nonsense, and nobody will say a word."

"Good idea!" said Mouse. "Let's go!"

Charlie shouted, "Scuzzawuzza Wop Wop Bootle-buttle!"

Mouse shouted, "Snackity-wackity BLORRRRRRRRRRRP!"

Nobody said a word.

It began to rain.

"When you are invisible," said Charlie, "you can take off all your clothes and dance and dance in the rain."

"Let's do it!" said Mouse.

Charlie and Mouse took off their clothes.

They danced and danced.

It was muddy and fun.

Then Ms. Margaret ran
past with an umbrella.
"Hi, Charlie!" shouted
Ms. Margaret. "Hi, Mouse!
It looks like you are having
a fun time."

ANIMALS

Charlie and Mouse were taking a bath.

Their animals were helping.

"Hello?" called Mom.

"Hello," said Charlie.

"Hello," said Mouse.

"I want to say I'm sorry," said Mom.

"What are you sorry for?"

asked Charlie.

"I should not have told you to *scram*,"

said Mom. "That was not nice.

I was feeling cranky."

"That is okay," said Charlie. "Scramming

was fun. We are fine."

"But we are also hungry," said Mouse.

"And so are the animals."

"Which animals?" asked Mom.

"*All* the animals!" said Mouse. "See?"

"Oh!" said Mom. "They do look hungry."

"They *are* hungry," said Mouse. "Especially the tigers. Tigers are always hungry."

"Well," said Mom. "We are having potpie for dinner."

"Tigers love potpie!" said Charlie.

Charlie and Mouse dried off.

They gathered up *all* the animals.

Mom found fourteen more plates.

And EVERYONE had dinner.

"Mom?" said Mouse, tucking his napkin into his lap.

"Yes?" said Mom.

"We want you to know, the animals like being included," said Mouse.

"Yes," said Charlie. "They are using their best table manners. Even the tigers."

"That is true," said Mouse. "And tigers have a hard time with table manners."

"Tigers," said Dad, "are not the only ones."

MORE MAGIC

Dad was cleaning up.

He washed the pots.

He washed the pans.

He washed the forks and spoons.

"Dad!" said Mouse. "You did not throw away

my magic potion, did you?"

"Is *that* your magic potion?"

asked Dad.

"Can't you tell?" said Mouse.

"How does it work?" asked Dad.

"I just put a drop of the potion on the tip of my nose," said Mouse. "Then I make a wish."

"Nifty!" said Dad. "Can I try it?"

"Sure," said Mouse.

Mouse put a drop of the potion on his nose.

Charlie put a drop of the potion on his nose.

Dad put a drop of the potion on his nose, too.

Mouse waited.

Charlie waited.

Dad washed more dishes.

"What did you wish for, Mouse?"

asked Charlie.

"I do not think I am supposed to tell anyone," said Mouse.

"Well, I do not think MY wish is happening," said Charlie. "I do not see any hamsters."

"Maybe the potion only works when it wants to," said Mouse.

"Or maybe it goes stale," said Charlie.

"You might be right," said Mouse.

"That is too bad."

"Oh, well," said Mouse. "We can always make more tomorrow!"

"Good thinking," said Charlie. "Let's go to bed, so tomorrow can come soon."

Charlie went to bed.

Mouse went to bed.

The house was very quiet.

Mom came into the kitchen.

"Why is the house so quiet?" she asked.

Dad smiled. "I got my wish!"

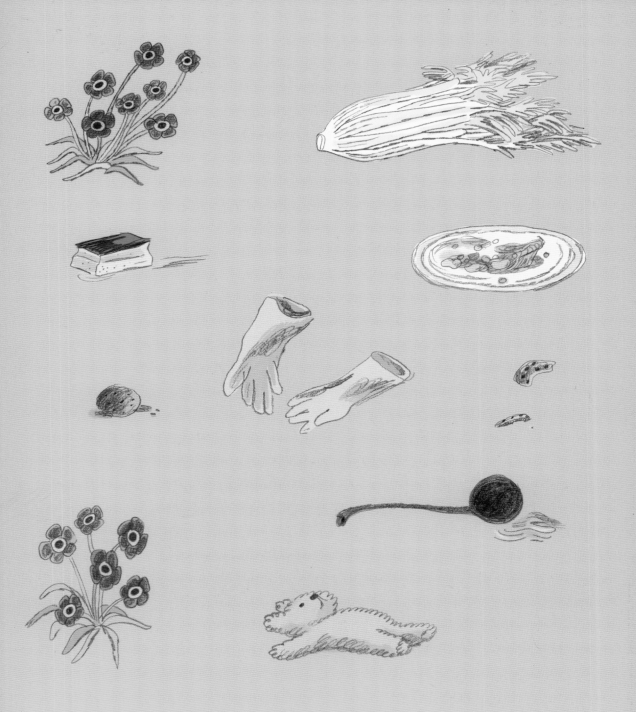